JOURNEY *of* FOREST FRIENDS

Colleen A. McGarr

Journey of Forest Friends
Copyright © 2021 by Colleen A. McGarr

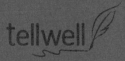

Tellwell Talent
www.tellwell.ca

ISBN
978-0-2288-3857-9 (Paperback)

Acknowledgement:

This story is dedicated to all the amazing people who reach out to help friends in need.

In memory of my beloved parents Marty and Kathy. They inspired me to become an author and encouraged me to always believe in myself.

"Mr. Bear, it's time to wake up it's a beautiful autumn day!" Sammy the squirrel whispered gently. Mr. Bear lifted his droopy eyelids. He noticed Sammy throwing acorns at his head. Looking through the cave he could see colorful leaves blowing in the wind.

"Thank goodness you woke me!"

"Come on, we have to go to the Fall party at Ruby the rabbit's house. Everyone is to bring something that makes them happy to share with the party guests." Said Sammy.

"I don't know what I could bring." Said Mr. Bear.

"Maybe you can find something along the way." Said Sammy as he jumped up and down with excitement.

The two walked deep into the forest where they spotted Tom the Turtle. He was carrying acorns on top of his shell. Sammy walked over to Tom. "Why are you carrying those acorns?"

"Well, I'm going to Ruby's party. It might take me a long time to get there." Said Tom with a grin. He slowly walked deeper into the forest as several brown acorns fell off his shell.

Next, they passed Ron the raccoon crossing a pond. He was dragging a large garbage can full of food. "I can't wait to go to the Fall party. I know that I will win because I have the biggest gift." Ron pulled the garbage can deeper into the forest.

"It doesn't matter what you bring as long as it makes you happy." Said Sammy.

Mr. Bear shouted, "I have an idea!" He started to climb up the tall oak tree. "Just look at that beautiful red apple growing on the tree."

"Wait Mr. Bear, please be careful! The tree branches are very weak and could break easily", explained Sammy.

As soon as Mr. Bear reached the top of the tree a branch snapped in half.

"Help!" Mr. Bear shouted as he started to fall. Just then another branch wrapped around his ankles. "I'm upside down! I don't know what to do!"

Sammy leaped onto the lowest branch. He climbed up the oak tree until he reached Mr. Bear's legs. Mr. Bear was too big to carry, so Sammy had to think fast. He quickly gathered leaves and threw them into a pile. Mr. Bear then fell from the tree. Sammy helped brush the dirt and leaves from Mr. Bear.

"Are you alright Mr. Bear?" asked Sammy. "Oh, yes I sure am," Said Mr. Bear with a smile.

"Boy, I wish we can find something to share at the party." Said Sammy.

Sammy stretched his tail and reached for the stars before he gently sat on the rock.

"No! Don't sit there!" Yelled bear as loud as he could.

Mr. Bear jumped and grabbed Sammy's tail.

"Ouch! What are you doing?" Screamed Sammy.

"I'm saving you from falling off the cliff! Look out!" Yelled Mr. Bear.

Mr. Bear grabbed Sammy's tail just in time. The dirt and rocks started to slide down off the cliff.

"You saved me Mr. Bear!" Cried Sammy!

"You saved each other." Said Dawn the deer looking up from drinking water by the stream.

"A true friendship is when you care for one another by listening and helping." Said Dawn.

It was starting to get dark. The full moon peaked through the trees. Sammy and Mr. Bear finally reached Ruby rabbit's house. Several friends of the forest were already at the party. Ruby was sitting on the porch sipping honey tea from a cup.

"Well good evening friends," Said Ruby as she lifted herself off the porch step. "Come on inside my house. I am making an apple pie, and I would love for you to try a slice. My grandmother rabbit use to make me this delicious dessert when I was little. It always makes me happy inside. Did you bring something that makes you happy?"

"I sure did!" Said Mr. Bear looking at Sammy with a smile. Sammy reached out and grabbed Mr. Bear's giant paw.

Mr. Bear and Sammy did not end up finding anything to bring to the party after all.

"It's not what you have, it's who you have that can make you happy. A true friend is around to help and laugh with you every step of the way. That is the greatest gift anyone should receive." Said Mr. Bear.

Sammy looked up at Mr. Bear and smiled.

CPSIA information can be obtained
at www.ICGtesting.com
Printed in the USA
LVHW070343220322
714057LV00002B/29